A Doll Named Fannie

Story and art photography by

Nancy B. Brewer

with illustrations by
Deena Bost

A Doll Named Fannie

Nancy B. Brewer

PUBLISHED BY:
BRENTWOOD PUBLISHERS GROUP
COLUMBUS, GEORGIA 31904
WWW.BRENTWOODBOOKS.COM

This little book is dedicated
to special young woman,
Kelly Rish
whose bright smile
makes this world a better
place in which to live.

Acknowledgments

I would like to express my great appreciation to my husband, Vernon and to my neighbor and good friend, Joann for all their help and support.

Introduction

A Doll Named Fannie, is a touching story told in the voice of Fannie, a German doll, who travels to Ireland to become little Molly O'Brien's faithful companion.

Like many of the Irish, hard times had fallen on Molly O'Brien's family. The great potato famine and the spread of disease had left Ireland starving and battling to survive. Beginning in 1845, Irish families were willing to risk their lives, traveling in death trap ships to come to America in search of the Great Land of Milk And Honey.

Unfortunately, they soon discovered the cities were already overcrowded with poor and desperate Irish immigrants. They were scorned because of their Catholic faith and shunned by those who feared they were spreading infectious diseases. Housing and jobs were scarce. Parents were forced to take undesirable and high-risk jobs. Many perished from disease, leaving behind their orphaned and abandoned children wandering the streets.

Organizations such as The Children's Aid Society and the New York Foundling Hospital structured a placing out program known as the "Baby Trains." Children were boarded upon these trains and at various stops offered up for adoption. Sadly, brothers and sisters were forever separated and older children became indentured servants. These train children were America's first, "Foster Children."

Between 1854 and 1929, approximately 200,000 children were placed out as a result of the orphan train movement.

"A Doll Named Fannie," is not just a story for children, but for all of us who respect the past, trust in the future and believe in the power of the imagination.

Nancy B. Brewer
April 28, 2010

Concord, North Carolina

I was manufactured or born, as I prefer to say, in the year 1859. My creation took place in Limbach, Germany. I was named, "Fannie."

Once the artist skillfully painted on my make-up, I was dressed in such a fine silk dress that even Queen Victoria would have been envious.

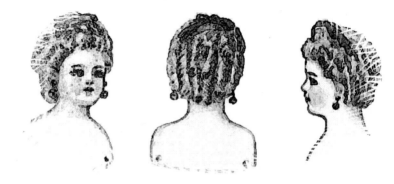

Just two days later, I was carefully packed in sawdust and placed in a small cedar box. I heard the voices of the other dolls calling to me as I was carried away. It was dark and lonely in the box.

I could smell the ocean and I was sure I was on a ship. Someone said we were heading for Ireland. By and by, the motion finally stopped. I heard a man's voice say, "I am Sean O'Brien. Has me package been delivered?"

"Yes, sir!" came another man's voice.

At once, I was lifted up and carried away. I could hear horses' hooves clicking and I knew I was traveling in a carriage. The ride was bumpy and hard and I was afraid my legs would be broken.

Next, I remember hearing children's voices and laughter. People were singing and there was jolly music outside the world of my little box.

Slowly, the hinges began to creak and my box opened. I saw two sparkly green eyes looking down at me, which belonged to a little girl with curly red hair.

Very gently, she lifted me out of the box. I was very quiet. She turned me around and then upside down to examine me. She seemed to like what she saw and so did I.

The man's voice called out, "How do you like your new dolly?"

Then the sweetest sound I had ever heard came out of the little girl's lips. "Papa is she mine...all mine...my very own?"

"Yes, Molly Grace O'Brien, she is all yours."

The little girl read the tag on my arm. "Her name is Fannie, but I think she needs a proper name. I will call her Frances, Frances O'Brien, and Fannie will be her pet name."

From that splendid day on, Molly and I were best friends. We were inseparable. Molly and I always played tea party and she dressed me in clothes she made herself, especially hats. She liked for me to wear hats.

All was well in our world until I heard Momma and Papa talking one night after Molly was asleep. I was not sure what a potato was, but I could tell it was something very important. Mother said they were all rotting and the people did not have enough to eat. People were sick and some were dying.

Momma cried and Papa walked the floor.

Then one day, Momma did not wake up. Molly was very sad. I did not wear a hat that day and we did not have a tea party. We cried.

Not long after that, Papa took us away. Again, I was to ride on a big ship. It was dirty and cold and Molly was hungry. She cried every night until she fell asleep, but I stayed awake to protect her if one of the big old rats climbed up on our little bed.

At last, we arrived at what I was to learn was New York City. Molly and I did not like this place. We moved into our new home, which was really just one room in a big apartment building. It was crowded with folks like us. The people were cranky and there were no green meadows where we could run and play.

Papa now had a job working in a factory and Molly and I stayed with a woman in the next room. She had a mean voice and Molly and I did not like her. Molly cried because she was always hungry and cold.

Papa did not come home from the factory one day. The woman said there had been an accident and Molly was now an orphan. Molly cried as the woman packed her things and took us to the Abbey.

I did not think it was so bad at the Nuns' home. Molly had little meat sandwiches to eat and there was always a nice warm fire. The other little girls asked Molly to play with them, but Molly was too sad to play games.

I recall a dreadful thing happening there one night. One of the other little girls came in and stole me from Molly's bed. I tried to call out, but Molly was asleep and did not hear me. I was very much afraid. Happily, the next day, the big important Nun found me and returned me to Molly. I was thankful because I knew Molly needed me.

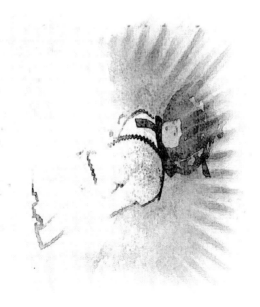

Shortly afterwards, the big important Nun said she was taking all the children on a train. Molly had to pack all her things; we were not coming back here to stay. We had never ridden on a train and Molly was nervous. I thought the train ride was exciting, but Molly was scared, so I decided to be scared too. Every time the train stopped, the children put on a parade so folks at the station could take a look at them. Strangely, some of the children never got back on the train.

Then one day it happened. We stopped at the station and I heard the conductor say, "All out for Salisbury, North Carolina." Molly and I got out to be in the parade. This time, a handsome lady came over and picked up Molly. The lady was wearing a little hat with a long blue feather that was the same color as her eyes. "What is your name?" she asked.

"Me name is Molly Grace O'Brien," said Molly, loud and clear.

Then the lady asked, "Molly, how would you like to come home with me and be my little girl?"

I tried to scream out as loud as I could, "Say yes, Molly!"

Molly studied the woman's face and I held my breath. At last, Molly said, "Yes."

The woman was so happy and tears shone in her eyes. The big important Nun told Molly "goodbye" and we rode away in a carriage. Molly did not cry, but she was very quiet.

When the carriage stopped, we saw a house with a big front porch. The woman who asked Molly to call her "Momma" took us upstairs to a little room. The room smelled sweet, like fresh flowers, and white lace curtains hung on the windows. I particularly liked the little bed, which was just Molly's size. "This is your room Molly," the new Momma said.

There were other dolls there, but I was not jealous. I was glad to have friends. The new Momma was very good to us. She baked bread and cookies and Molly and I got new clothes. After a little while, we were having tea parties and I was wearing hats again.

Later we met a Grandpa and Grandma. Molly and I heard them say our new Momma's husband was killed in the war between the states. We did not know what a war was, but sometimes late at night we heard the Momma crying. We did not ask why, but somehow we just understood.

Summers turned into Falls and Winters into Springs and Molly grew up.

She sat me up on a shelf where my new job was to watch her put on perfumes, comb her hair and look in the mirror. We stopped playing tea parties and I wore the same hat every day.

John started visiting about the same time Molly began wearing fancy hats. She said they were in love and they were going to get married. I sat on a pillow and watched the wedding. Molly was beautiful in her long white dress. She cried, but I did not think she was sad.

So, we moved again, to a new house with John. Molly kissed John often. She was always busy with real tea parties and big girl work. Even though I was just left to sit on the shelf, I was happy because Molly was happy.

After about a year, something wonderful happened! A baby girl was born. I was delighted to hear her name was Frances, too. Molly sat me upon a shelf in the baby's room. I now had the important job of watching over the baby day and night; I was so proud. She was a special baby and Molly and I shared her. Molly sang to her at night, just like she used to sing to me. I sang along softly.

In no time, Frances was walking and talking. She reminded me so much of Molly when she was a little girl. Molly showed her how to play tea party and I showed her how nice I looked in hats.

Dear little Frances was not as gentle as Molly and she cost me quite a few scars. I did not mind too much, because those were the grandest days of my life. Just me, Molly, and our little girl.

The years flew by and just like Molly, Frances grew up and got married. Before Frances had her own baby, she came to see us every Sunday. Once she moved to Charlotte, she rarely came.

From time to time, Molly would come and sit in Frances's room. She was sad and we both missed Frances. I would have been happy to play tea party, if she would have just taken me down off the shelf.

One of those days, she came for me and placed me back on the shelf in her room. Some nights she would take me down and sing to me, but it was not as it used to be.

The days passed and I watched over her as she took her afternoon naps. Her curly red hair was silver now, but she was still beautiful to me.

I would have had no warning at all, had I not heard Molly talking on her new telephone. I was excited; we were moving to Concord where Frances lived.

A day or so later, some people came and packed all of Molly's things in boxes, her fancy hats, her perfume bottles and even her silver handled hairbrush.

As they packed up the last of dear Molly's things, I was sure I was going to be left there alone. Suddenly, I heard a familiar voice. It was Frances. "Here I am!" I called out to her, but she did not look up at me.

She stood in the middle of the empty room, took out her handkerchief and wiped her eyes.

As Frances turned to leave, I called out again, but she never looked back.

A bald headed man with a big fat belly came in next and rolled up the rug. "Hey," he called out to another one of the working men. "How about this old doll, reckon it's worth anything?"

A voice from the other room answered, "Are you kidding? In the condition she is in, she is not worth a dime. I'd just throw her in the trash."

I heard it. It was true; I was just a broken down old doll, not worth a dime.

The man reached up with his dirty fingers and pulled me off the shelf. Then he shoved me in a box, even though I was old and fragile.

I cannot say how long I was in that box: Perhaps ten, twenty or fifty years. All I did was sleep and try to dream of the happy days with Molly.

Then one day, the box opened and there was light again! I saw the face of a nice lady smiling at me. She held me up and gently stroked my head. It was almost like the first time Molly saw me. She whispered to me, **"Hello, Old Girl, I am going to take you home with me. You remind me of the doll Grandma Molly used to have."**

A word from the author

It is my greatest desire that my historical fiction works will encourage all my readers to listen to the voices of long ago, take pride in their own ancestors' accomplishments, find strength in their suffering and learn from the past.

"A glance to the past, allows us to see the path clearly ahead."

Nancy B. Brewer

About the author:

Ms. Brewer is a native of North Carolina. She is a storyteller and history reenactor. Brewer, is known for her soft southern style and a master of weaving historically accurate stories, both for adults and children.

Carolina Rain

Beyond Sandy Ridge –
(The sequel to Carolina Rain)

Quotes and Poems in Black and White

To order books or schedule an appearance please visit the author's website:
www.nancybbrewer.com